Secret Kingdom

Special thanks to Liss Norton

For D.S. with lots of love

ORCHARD BOOKS

First published in Great Britain in 2013 by Orchard Books
This edition published in 2016 by The Watts Publishing Group

3 5 7 9 10 8 6 4

© 2013 Hothouse Fiction Limited
Illustrations © Orchard Books 2013

A CIP catalogue record for this book is available from the British Library.

ISBN 978 1 40832 338 0

Printed in Great Britain by Clays Ltd, St Ives plc

The paper and board used in this book are made from wood from responsible sources

Orchard Books
An imprint of Hachette Children's Group
Part of The Watts Publishing Group Limited
Carmelite House, 50 Victoria Embankment, London EC4Y 0DZ

An Hachette UK Company
www.hachette.co.uk
www.hachettechildrens.co.uk

Series created by Hothouse Fiction
www.hothousefiction.com

Wildflower Wood

ROSIE BANKS

ORCHARD

This is the
Secret Kingdom

Wildflower Wood

Contents

An Amazing Surprise

"Look how long this is!" exclaimed Jasmine Smith. She held up the daisy chain she was making. "I'm going to turn it into a necklace for Summer. Butterflies will love her!"

"She'll like that!" Ellie Macdonald giggled as she flopped down on Jasmine's lawn. Their friend Summer Hammond loved all animals, and Ellie knew she'd be pleased to have butterflies fluttering all around her.

"Where is she anyway?" Jasmine asked. "She should have been here half an hour ago." She looked down her long, narrow garden, past the flowerbeds and the old apple tree to the back gate, but there was no sign of their friend. Laying the daisy chain carefully on the lawn, she sprinted down the garden, her long black hair streaming out behind her. "I'll see if she's coming," she called over her shoulder.

Ellie put her daisy chain beside Jasmine's and skipped after her. "I hope she gets here soon," she said, tucking a loose strand of curly red hair behind one ear.

Jasmine opened the gate, then jumped back as Summer raced up on her bike, her blonde pigtails flying. "Sorry I'm late," she panted. "I was looking for my fairytale book. I can't find it anywhere, and I'd promised my brother Finn I'd read him a story from it. He was really disappointed."

"Oh no!" said Ellie. "Can you remember where you had it last?"

Summer leaned her bike against the fence, then followed Ellie and Jasmine back up the garden. "I know I had it at the Summer Ball." She lowered her voice. "When we were…you-know-where."

The three friends exchanged excited

glances, thinking about the amazing magical secret they all shared.

Jasmine gasped. "Did you leave it—"

"In the Secret Kingdom?" Ellie finished for her in a whisper, not wanting to be overheard. They were the only people who knew about King Merry's magical world and the girls wanted to keep it that way. When the Secret Kingdom had been in trouble, King Merry's Magic Box had found the only three people who could help – Summer, Jasmine and Ellie. Now his pixie assistant, Trixi, sent them magical messages through the Magic Box whenever they were needed.

Just the mention of the Secret Kingdom sent a tingle down Summer's spine. It was a wonderful place full of elves, mermaids and other magical creatures.

"Remember the dream dragons?" Ellie said excitedly.

"And the bubblebees," added Summer. "They were so sweet!"

"I wish we could go back," Jasmine sighed. "We haven't been there for ages."

"I wonder how Trixi is," Ellie thought out loud.

"It would be great to hear from her," Jasmine agreed.

"But it's sort of a good thing that we haven't heard," Summer pointed out. "Trixi only sends us a message if Queen Malice is up to something. And as we haven't heard from her, that must mean everything's okay there."

Queen Malice, King Merry's sister, wanted to rule the kingdom, and she was always causing trouble. She'd even tried to turn the kindly king into a stink toad, one of the nastiest, pongiest creatures in the whole kingdom! The girls had had to collect six rare ingredients from around the kingdom to make the counter-potion to turn King Merry back to his normal jolly self.

"I know," said Jasmine, "but I wish we could go back. I miss Trixi and King Merry."

"Me too," said Ellie and Summer together.

"And I'd love to see the unicorns again." Summer sighed.

"Queen Malice was banished to the Troll Territories when we were there last," Ellie reminded them. "So that's probably why we haven't heard anything. King Merry took away her thunderbolt staff too. She won't be able to do anything bad without it."

"I keep checking the Magic Box all the same," Jasmine said. "But there haven't been any messages."

"I suppose we'll just have to be patient and wait until we hear from Trixi again," Ellie said. She picked up her daisy chain and rested it on her curly hair like a crown. "This will have to do until I can wear my real tiara again," she added, laughing.

"Can I have a look in your room, Jasmine, just in case I left my fairytale book here?" Summer asked.

"Course you can," Jasmine said. "Do you need a hand?"

Summer giggled. Jasmine didn't have that many books – she preferred reading music magazines because she wanted to be a pop star when she grew up. "No, thanks. I think I can manage!" she teased.

"It's lucky it won't take you long to look," Jasmine said, grinning. "It's too sunny to be indoors today."

Summer ran inside and upstairs to Jasmine's bedroom. The Magic Box stood on Jasmine's bedside table next to a framed picture of a dancer that Ellie had painted for Jasmine's birthday. Summer peered into the mirror on the lid, hoping she'd see a message there, but all she saw was her own reflection looking back at her thoughtfully.

Sighing, she quickly searched Jasmine's shelves, but her missing fairytale book wasn't there.

As she turned towards the door, a flash of light caught her eye. Glancing round hurriedly, she saw that glittery light was pouring from the Magic Box's mirror. "A message!" she gasped. "At last!"

She grabbed the box and raced downstairs and out into the garden.

Hearing her running footsteps, Jasmine and Ellie looked up from their daisy chains. "Did you find your—?" began Ellie, then she spotted the Magic Box under Summer's arm and sprang to her feet. "Is there a message?"

"Yes!" Summer placed the Magic Box on the lawn and they all kneeled around it, peering into the glowing mirror. At

once, a riddle appeared there in curly
writing.

Jasmine read it out:

"Pink walls and ruby turrets high,
With gold spires reaching to the sky.
Please come, dear friends.
Remember how?
And pay us all a visit now."

"Pink walls…" breathed Summer.

"And ruby turrets and gold spires!" Ellie exclaimed, her eyes shining. "There's only one place that can be!"

Eagerly, the three girls placed their hands over the green gems. "King Merry's Enchanted Palace!" they cried together.

The Magic Box flew open and a jet of brilliant, silvery light shot out. Rainbow-coloured sparkles went whirling round the girls like a mini-tornado. Then the tornado slowed and a beautiful pixie appeared, flying on a leaf. She had pointy ears that peeked out from a tangle of blonde hair, and she was wearing a rose-petal hat, a dress made from pale green leaves and cute petal shoes. On one finger, her magical pixie ring glittered brightly.

"Trixi!" the girls cheered.

"Girls! It's so good to see you again," cried Trixi, beaming at them all. She flew to each of them in turn and kissed the tips of their noses. "I've missed you."

"We've missed you too, Trixi," Summer said.

"What's happening in the Secret Kingdom?" asked Jasmine.

Trixi steered her leaf down and hovered just above the Magic Box. "Queen Malice has just come back from the Troll Territories," she said.

"That sounds like trouble," Ellie said anxiously.

"That was what I thought, too," continued Trixi. "But something amazing has happened." She looked around at them all, smiling broadly. "Queen Malice has turned good!"

The Missing Book

"I don't believe it!" gasped Jasmine.

"It's true," Trixi said, still smiling. "But I thought you'd like to see for yourselves after all the trouble she's caused."

"Yes, please!" the girls cried together. They grabbed one another's hands and held tight, ready for the magical journey to the Secret Kingdom.

Trixi tapped the Magic Box with her ring and chanted:

"Pixie magic, lift us high;
To the palace let us fly!"

As she spoke, her words appeared on
the box's mirror. They grew brighter and
brighter, then disappeared up into the sky
in a whirling stream of vivid pink sparkles.
Ellie, Jasmine and Summer squeezed one
another's hands tight as they spun up into
the air. "Here we go!" cried Jasmine. "Off
to the Secret Kingdom again! Yippee!"

The magic swirled them up into a

velvety purple sky full of twinkling silver
stars. "Lovely!" Summer breathed, gazing
around in wonder. Then the magical
whirlwind slowed and they saw that the
stars were glittering lights in the ceiling
of a grand hallway. They landed with a
gentle bump.

"We're here!" exclaimed Jasmine.
They all looked round at the room in
amazement. There were richly coloured
tapestries of unicorns and mermaids on
all the walls and the floor was made of
polished pink marble.

"This way," said Trixi, speeding away
on her leaf so quickly that the girls had
to sprint to keep up with her. "I can't
wait to show you!"

Ellie felt something settle on her head
as she ran. Raising her hand, she found

that the jewelled tiara that showed she
was a Very Important Friend to the
Secret Kingdom had magically appeared.
Jasmine and Summer were wearing theirs
too, and the gems cast long rainbows of
colour ahead of them across the marble
floor.

Soon they reached a pair of tall doors

carved with little crowns. "Welcome
to King Merry's grand throne room,"
announced Trixi. Turning the gold
handles, she opened the doors and
ushered them inside.

The throne room was enormous, with
walls covered in crimson wallpaper
swirled with gold twists and spirals.

A glittering chandelier hung from the ceiling, and the golden carpet felt thick and springy beneath the girls' feet.

A crowd of pixies, brownies, unicorns and other magical creatures was already there. They were chattering excitedly and craning their necks to see what was happening at the far end of the room where King Merry sat on his golden throne.

"There's Queen Malice!" gasped Summer.

"Now we'll see if she really has turned good," Jasmine said. It still didn't seem possible that the nasty queen could have changed so much.

"She looks different," Ellie pointed out.

The queen was standing meekly in front of King Merry, her head bowed

and her hands clasped behind her back.
She was wearing a long light-blue dress,
instead of her usual black, and her hair
was fastened into a neat bun on top of
her head. Her Storm Sprites stood quietly
behind her, their wings folded and their
faces solemn.

"Perhaps she really has changed," whispered kind-hearted Summer as they found a space in the crowd.

"And her Storm Sprites too," Ellie agreed. "I've never seen them behaving so well before."

"It's good to see the improvement in you, sister," said King Merry, smiling fondly at Queen Malice. "I never thought you'd be so nice. Especially after you tried to turn me into a stink toad!" He leaned forward and his crown fell off and clattered to the floor.

The Storm Sprites began to whisper eagerly, but Queen Malice frowned at them and they fell silent. She picked up the crown and handed it back to King Merry. "I'm sorry, brother," she said in a gentle voice. "I can see now that it was a wicked thing to do. My time in the Troll Territories has made me understand how wrong I was." She lifted her head and her gaze fell on her thunderbolt staff, which was being held by one of King Merry's elf butlers. For a moment her dark eyes gleamed eagerly, then she lowered her head again.

"I still don't trust her," whispered Jasmine. "Did you see the look in her eyes just then?"

King Merry stood up and put his chubby arm round his sister. "As a reward for changing into such a lovely person," he said, taking her staff from the elf butler, "you may have this back, dear sister. Think of the good you can do with your magic now!"

Ellie gasped as King Merry held out the

thunderbolt staff.

Summer crossed her fingers tightly.

"Wait—" Jasmine started, but it was too late.

Queen Malice snatched the staff from him. Cackling loudly, she held it high, sending thunderbolts zinging around the throne room. The watching crowd dived for cover, flinging themselves under tables and behind chairs and cupboards.

"Over here!" cried Trixi. She zoomed behind a pillar and Ellie, Summer and Jasmine dashed after her.

"I knew it was too good to be true," groaned Jasmine as they all peeked out.

"You fool, brother!" shrieked Queen Malice. The hairpins in her bun shot out and her black frizzy hair sprang free. "Did you really believe that I, Queen

Malice, could ever be good?"

One of her thunderbolts bounced off
the ceiling and sparks showered her dress,
turning it midnight-black. The Storm
Sprites spread their
bat-like wings
and soared
into the air,
sniggering
gleefully.

"Now to take over the kingdom!"
Queen Malice shrieked. She spun round
and pointed at a group of brownies
cowering behind a chair. "Soon you will
bow to me, not to my fool of a brother."

Trembling, the brownies huddled closer
together.

"The whole kingdom will do as I
say," cried the queen, "because only I
can protect you from what is about to
happen!"

Jasmine, Ellie and Summer exchanged
anxious looks. "What do you think she
means?" whispered Ellie. "What's about
to happen?"

Queen Malice shook her staff and a
black thundercloud began to grow in the
centre of the room. "I, Queen Malice,
am back!" she cried. Throwing back her

head, she screamed with laughter.

Howling delightedly, the Storm Sprites swarmed around her.

King Merry looked up at his sister in confusion. "Does this mean you haven't changed after all?" he asked, surprised.

"Of course I haven't changed!" she crowed. "Do you know how boring trolls are? All they talk about is rocks! And I was stuck with nothing to do but read this stupid book!" More sparks rained down and suddenly a book appeared in her hand.

Summer gasped. "My fairytale book!"

"Now you can all share the stories I read," cackled the queen. She pointed her staff at the book and another thunderbolt shot out with a deafening crack. "Once upon a time," she cried, "a beautiful queen let loose a group of fairytale baddies in a place called the Secret Kingdom!"

Into the Woods

The fairytale book flew up into the air
and its pages fluttered wildly. A wolf
sprang out of the book. Behind him
came a green-faced witch dressed all in
black and flying on a broomstick. Then
an enormous hand with fingers like
rolling pins appeared.

"What's that?" Ellie quavered.

The thundercloud grew bigger still, filling the entire throne room with a darkness so deep that the girls couldn't see anything at all. Queen Malice's voice echoed though the cloud as she laughed louder and louder. "These villains will ruin the kingdom bit by bit until you're begging me to rule!" she cackled.

With a final crash of thunder, the room fell silent. When the cloud cleared, Queen Malice, her Storm Sprites and the fairytale villains had all vanished.

"We've got to stop them!" cried Jasmine as the girls and Trixi came out from behind the pillar.

The pixies, elves, unicorns and other creatures crept out of their hiding places looking dazed and unhappy. Some of the elves were crying and the brownies put their arms round them kindly, whispering words of comfort.

"We need to find out which baddies Queen Malice has released," Summer said. Her fairytale book was lying on the floor nearby and she picked it up.

"Which baddies are in there?" asked Ellie, peering over her shoulder as she flipped through the pages.

"There's a wolf, for a start," groaned Summer. She held up the book and they all saw a blank wolf-shaped space in one of the pictures.

"I thought I spotted a wolf on the thundercloud," Ellie said. "And didn't a witch fly out too?"

Summer flicked through some more pages. "There," she said, pointing to a picture of the inside of a dingy cottage where an empty shape was hunched over a cauldron. "The witch should be here."

"I think a giant came out of the book too." Jasmine gulped. "I'm sure I saw a massive hand, but then the cloud got too big and I couldn't see anything else."

Nervously, Summer turned to a story about a bad-tempered giant. "He's gone too," she confirmed. "And there's an evil dragon missing as well," she added, turning over more pages. "And a wizard!"

Ellie shivered. "Are there any others?"

she asked anxiously.

"An ogre," Summer said. She flicked
to the end of the book. "That's all of
them."

"That's enough!" exclaimed Ellie. "I
think—" She broke off as she noticed a
tiny ball of light speeding towards them.
"What's that?" she gasped, ducking as it
zoomed over her head.

"Don't worry, it's only a glow-worm
messenger," Trixi replied.
She held out her hand
and the glow-worm
sped towards her,
its wings beating
furiously. It
hovered beside her
ear and whispered
something.

"Thank you," said Trixi when he'd finished.

"Good luck!" squeaked the glow-worm. It circled around them all, then flew out of an open window and away.

"What did he say, Trixi?" asked Summer. She wished the glow-worm had stayed a bit longer so she could have had a good look at him. She'd never seen one before.

"He brought a message from the gnomes in Wildflower Wood," Trixi replied. "It's under attack!"

"It must be one of the fairytale baddies," said Jasmine. "But which one?"

"We should go at once," Trixi said urgently.

"Hang on, let's say hello to King Merry first," said Ellie. The king looked very unhappy, slumped in his throne with his head in his hands. "It might cheer him up a bit if he knows we're here."

The girls raced across to him. "Don't worry, Your Majesty," said Jasmine. "We'll put things right."

King Merry sat up straight and his face brightened. "Ellie! Summer! Jasmine!" he exclaimed. Then he slumped down again. "Did you see what happened?" he groaned. "My sister... I can't believe that she could..." He sighed heavily. "I really thought she'd changed."

"She did look different at first," said Summer kindly. "She fooled everyone."

The king nodded glumly. "Thank goodness you're here! I'm afraid we're going to need all the help you can give us," he said.

"Don't worry, Your Majesty," Ellie replied. "We're on our way to help the gnomes who live in Wildflower Wood right now." She twisted the ends of her hair nervously. "And we ought to get going straight away."

"The gnomes?" King Merry looked bewildered. "Is something wrong with them?"

"We think there's a fairytale baddie there," explained Jasmine.

"Poor things." King Merry sighed. He looked at them gravely. "You will be careful, won't you?"

"Of course we will," promised Ellie. "Now let's go!"

Trixi stretched out her hand. Her pixie ring glittered on her finger and she tapped it and called out:

"Brave helpers, now you must not fail,
Return these villains to their fairytale!"

Jasmine, Ellie and Summer held hands as pink sparkles flew out of the ring, then fluttered gently down to surround them. A moment later, the girls were lifted off their feet. Suddenly they found themselves in a forest surrounded by hundreds of towering flower stems that swayed gently in the soft breeze. Each stem was topped with a brightly coloured flower, and enormous butterflies fluttered around them, their wings glittering in the sunlight.

"What an amazing place!" cried Summer, gazing up at a flower with massive pink-edged petals. "These flowers are as big as trees!"

Ellie took a deep breath. "And they smell fantastic," she said. "Kind of like roses, chocolate and lavender all mixed up together."

"Wildflower Wood is part of Flower Forest," Trixi explained. "All the flowers grow this big around here."

"We looked down on Flower Forest from Cloud Island," Jasmine said. "Do you remember? It was amazing then, but it's even better up close!" She flung out her arms. "Everything's enormous!"

"And look!" exclaimed Ellie. She ran to the stem of a flower with a mass of thin sunshine-yellow petals like a huge lion's mane. The base of the stem was very wide and there was a little green door and two windows set into it. A sign fixed above the door said:

Thistle's House

"I wonder who Thistle is?" Summer said excitedly.

The door began to creak open and Jasmine stepped back, pulling Ellie and Summer with her. "I think we're about to find out!" she gasped.

Fe, Fi, Fo, Fum!

Suddenly the door of the flower-stem house swung wide open and out came a small gnome with a bushy white beard, a blue pointed hat and the reddest cheeks and nose the girls had ever seen. He was carrying a wooden bucket with a long-handled spoon in it.

He smiled when he saw the girls. "How do you do?" he said politely, raising his hat. "I'm afraid I can't stop. Busy, busy, busy."

"Are you Thistle?" Ellie asked.

The gnome bowed. "Thistle, at your service," he said.

"I'm Jasmine," said Jasmine. "And this is Summer, Ellie and Trixi." The little pixie pirouetted on her leaf.

Thistle looked the girls over, staring at their tiaras, his eyes bright with interest. "Forgive me for asking, but are you humans?"

"Yes," the girls answered together.

"Well I never!" he exclaimed. "You're the first humans I've ever seen. Delighted! Really delighted!" Setting down his bucket, he shook hands with them all. "Now I really must be off." He glanced at his wrist and the girls saw a fluffy dandelion fastened to it. "My dandelion watch says it's gone eleven and I've got lots of sugarsap to collect."

He darted to the next flower and began to climb a long ladder that was propped against its stem.

"Wait! What's sugarsap?" Summer asked.

But Thistle had climbed so quickly that he was already out of earshot.

"The gnomes look after the wood and collect sugarsap from the flowers," explained Trixi. "It's the most amazing drink. All the children in the kingdom drink it and it helps them grow up big and strong."

"I'd like to try it," said Jasmine eagerly.

"Maybe once we've found our fairytale baddie," Ellie reminded her. "Bother, we should have asked Thistle if he'd seen anything strange."

They all looked up, but the little gnome had already reached the top of the ladder and climbed onto the flower's wide petals.

"He'd have mentioned something if he'd been attacked," said Summer. "And he didn't seem at all worried. Are you sure we've come to the right place, Trixi?"

"Flower Forest is so big that

they might not have heard about the baddie here yet," said Trixi.

Ellie looked around. There were little doors in lots of the flower stems, and the forest was wonderfully peaceful. She could hear bees buzzing high overhead and leaves rustling gently in the breeze. "I hope we manage to stop whoever it is before they spoil the forest," she said.

"Me too," agreed Jasmine. "It's lovely here."

"I wonder which baddie it is," said Summer, glancing around anxiously. She hoped none of them was lurking in the shadows.

"Let's have a look around and see if we can spot anything," Ellie suggested. She started down a narrow winding path that led between the flowers.

Jasmine and Summer followed her, and Trixi sped after them on her leaf. They hadn't gone far when they heard a shrill cry.

"What was that?" gasped Ellie, spinning round.

"I don't know," Summer replied. "But I'm pretty sure something's wrong. Look at the butterflies."

The butterflies had been drifting lazily from flower to flower. Now they went streaming away through the forest, their wings flapping furiously.

The girls stretched up on tiptoe, trying to see what had frightened them. Then they heard a shout.

"Run for your lives!" Thistle yelled as he scrambled down his ladder. "Run!" he repeated, charging over to them.

All around, gnomes were racing down from the tops of the flowers, sliding down the ladders as fast as they could. "It's coming!" they shrieked.

"What's coming?" asked Summer nervously.

The gnomes didn't reply. They disappeared into their houses, then peeped fearfully out of the windows.

"This way!" Thistle cried to the girls and Trixi. He raced to his house and threw open the door. "You'll be safe inside."

"Thanks, Thistle," said Jasmine bravely. "But we've got to get this... whatever-it-is...back into our fairytale book."

Thistle looked at them admiringly. "You're going to save us and our forest?" he asked.

"You bet!" the three girls exclaimed together. There was no way they'd let Queen Malice ruin the wonderful wood.

Thistle looked from his house to the girls. Then he smoothed down his white beard and squared his shoulders. "I'll help," he said bravely. He closed his front door, then came and stood beside them. The tip of his pointy hat only came up to Ellie's knees, but he looked fiercely determined. "No one's going to spoil our wood without a fight!"

He broke off suddenly as the ground began to shake. Then they heard a terrible crashing sound coming from the forest. "It's an earthquake!" squeaked Trixi in terror. She clung tightly to her leaf as the flowers all around began to sway and tremble.

"Fe, fi, fo, fum," boomed a thunderous voice. It sounded deep and fierce and scary. The girls looked at one another anxiously.

"What's that?" cried Thistle, pointing up into the flower tops, his finger shaking as a huge head came into view. It had a shock of shaggy brown hair, a mouth as wide as a train tunnel, enormous grey eyes and a fat red nose like a massive tomato.

"It's not an earthquake," Ellie gasped. "It's footsteps – giant footsteps!"

A Giant Problem!

The girls watched, horrified, as the giant barged through the forest, knocking over flowers and ladders as he passed. "All that sugarsap going to waste," wailed Thistle, shaking his fist up at the giant.

"And so many homes being smashed," Summer added sadly as another flower fell. She hoped nobody was inside.

"Look out!" shouted Jasmine as a tall purple flower came crashing down towards them.

Hearts thudding wildly, they leapt out of the way just in time.

"That was close," Ellie gasped.

"How can we stop him?" groaned Thistle. "He's destroying everything." He gazed mournfully at the golden liquid that was spilling out of the fallen flower. "If only I had my bucket," he sighed.

"Hey!" Jasmine called, cupping her hands around her mouth. "Mr Giant!"

The giant went on stamping through the forest, breaking more flowers with every step.

"I don't think he can hear you," said Summer. "Let's all shout together."

"Good idea," agreed Ellie and Jasmine.

"One, two, three..." Summer chanted.

"Giant!" they all yelled as loudly as they could.

The giant still didn't hear them.

"Oh, this is hopeless," sighed Ellie.

"He's too tall to hear us down here on the ground." She couldn't bear to see the damage the giant was causing. Every step he took broke more flowers, smashing more of the gnomes' houses and leaving puddles of sugarsap soaking into the ground.

"I'll see what I can do," Trixi said. She steered her leaf towards the giant's head.

"Be careful, Trixi!" Summer called after her.

They watched anxiously as Trixi circled the giant's enormous head, then hovered beside his massive ear.

"Please stop," she begged in her loudest voice. "You're breaking all the flowers."

The giant looked round at Trixi for a second, then raised a massive hand and swatted her away as though she were an annoying, buzzing fly.

"Trixi!" Summer gasped as the leaf went somersaulting through the air with Trixi lying flat on it, clinging on desperately with both hands.

The girls watched in dismay as the little pixie's leaf fell. Somehow Trixi was managing to keep it the right way up, but it was spinning round and round, out of control.

Jasmine rushed forward, her hands cupped, ready to catch Trixi if she fell off.

"Look how fast she's going!" cried Summer. Trixi was zooming towards the ground at a terrifying speed. "She's going to crash!"

"She's trying to stand up!" Ellie gasped. They watched fearfully as Trixi wobbled to her feet. She stretched out her arms to steady the leaf.

"She's done it!" cheered Jasmine as the leaf slowed down.

Summer sighed in relief and Ellie let out a deep breath. "Well done, Trixi!" she grinned.

Trixi steered her leaf over to them.

"Are you okay?" Summer asked as the leaf stopped in front of them. The little pixie looked horribly pale and her legs were shaking.

"Yes, I think so," Trixi replied, smoothing down her dress and flipping her hair out of her eyes. "But it was pretty scary for a while." She looked around at them anxiously. "We've got to find a way of stopping that mean giant."

"How about tripping him up?" suggested Jasmine. "That would stop him all right."

"But it would be terrible for Wildflower Wood," said Thistle. "He'd squash even more flowers when he fell."

"Yes," cried a chorus of voices all around them. The gnomes had come out of their houses and were watching anxiously. "Please don't let him fall over and destroy our homes," they begged.

"We won't," promised Jasmine. "But we need to think of something else quickly."

They all concentrated hard, trying to come up with a new idea to stop the giant. He was so huge, what could they possibly do against someone so big?

"It's hopeless, isn't it?" groaned Thistle. "That dreadful giant is going to march right through the forest, breaking everything in his path."

"No, he's not," Summer replied determinedly. She went on, "We've solved problems for King Merry before. We can't let ourselves be beaten by one of Queen Malice's baddies, no matter how big he is!"

Just then the giant grabbed a flower, yanking it right out of the ground and making the gnomes gasp in horror. He held it to his mouth and tipped it upside down. "He's drinking our sugarsap!" cried Thistle indignantly.

"Stop it!" the gnomes yelled, jumping up and down. But the giant tossed the flower aside and pulled up another one.

"Soon there won't be any left for the children," Thistle said sadly.

"I've got it!" Ellie announced at last. "He's only breaking things because he's so big. Can you make him smaller, Trixi?"

"Of course!" Jasmine cried. "If he's smaller he won't be able to pull up flowers or trample on them."

"And we'll be able to get him back into the book," added Summer eagerly.

"Good idea!" Trixi grinned. She thought for a second, then tapped her ring and chanted:

"This giant's bigger than a tree.
Let's make him small as small can be!"

A stream of pink sparkles flew from

Trixi's ring. They surrounded the
giant, then closed in tight around him.
He tried to bat them away, but as his
hand touched them he began to shrink.
Letting the flower fall, he looked around
in confusion. "What's happening?" he
boomed in a voice so loud that it made
the forest shake.

"Well done, Trixi!" exclaimed Ellie as
the giant became smaller and smaller.

Soon he was much shorter than the
flowers, but still he went on shrinking
until they could see that his red-tomato
nose was covered in lumpy warts and
that his eyebrows met in the middle.
Down, down, down he shrank until his
head reached no higher than the girls'
waists.

"Fe, fi, fo, fum?" the little giant said

in a squeaky voice. He looked up at the girls, his grey eyes puzzled.

"You've come out of a fairytale book," Summer told him. She held up the book to show him.

The giant still looked confused. "How did I—?" he began.

"An evil queen put a spell on the book," explained Ellie.

"But you don't need to worry. We're going to put you back into your story," said Jasmine. Her hand flew to her mouth. "How, though?" she gasped. She looked at Ellie and Summer, horrified. "We don't know how to get the baddies back into the book!"

"We've got to find a way," said Summer determinedly.

"Is your magic strong enough to do it, Trixi?" Ellie asked.

"No," Trixi sighed. "I could make him small because Queen Malice hadn't cast a spell to make him big – he was already gigantic. But she did use her magic to bring him out of the book and I can't reverse that. Her spells are just too powerful for my magic to break."

"Try opening the book to the right page," Jasmine suggested. "Maybe that will give us a clue." They all watched as Summer flipped through the pages.

"Got it," said Summer. She opened the book wide so that they could all see the giant-shaped gap in the picture. At once, the book began to glow with yellow light. The light grew brighter, then slowly long strands began to reach out towards the giant.

The girls looked at one another, relieved. Any minute now the giant would be safely back inside the book and the first fairytale baddie would be caught.

But the giant backed away as the light inched towards him. Then, suddenly, he turned and started to run. "I'm not going back in there!" he squeaked. "I'm bored of being in the same old story. It's much more fun here!" The girls stared as he dashed away through the woods, his little legs moving fast as he wove through the trees.

"Come on!" cried Jasmine. "Don't let him get away!"

A Bird's-eye View

Ellie, Jasmine and Summer raced after the giant with Trixi zooming along beside them on her leaf. Behind them came Thistle and the other gnomes. "Come back, giant!" Jasmine yelled.

It was difficult to keep the giant in sight as he ran in circles and ducked behind the huge flower stalks. At last he disappeared completely.

"Where's he gone?" groaned Ellie. "We've got to catch him."

"Let's split up," suggested Jasmine. "I'll go this way." She raced away along a narrow path.

"Shout if you spot him," Summer called after her.

"I will! Good luck!" Jasmine called back.

Summer took a path that branched off to the left, Ellie went right and Trixi flew straight ahead.

The girls ran fast, looking all around, but there was no sign of the tiny giant.

"He must be here somewhere," Jasmine muttered as she dashed along. It would be terrible if Trixi's shrinking spell wore off and the giant grew big again. He'd already caused way too much damage.

There was a bend in the path ahead. Jasmine raced round it, then stopped suddenly. Ellie was heading her way. A moment later, Summer came bursting out of a clump of huge leaves. "Did you see the giant?" she panted.

Ellie and Jasmine shook their heads sadly.

"Neither did I," Trixi said, flying out from behind a thick flower stalk.

"What are we going to do?" asked Summer. "This forest is huge. He could be just about anywhere."

They heard footsteps behind them and spun round eagerly, hoping the giant was coming. But it was just Thistle, so out of breath that he could only plod. "Where...has...he...gone?" he puffed.

"We've lost him," Ellie sighed.

"What we need…is a…bird's-eye… view." Thistle pointed to one of the tall ladders. Looking up, the girls could see that it reached to the top of a beautiful orange flower.

"This is one… of the highest… flowers in the… forest," panted Thistle proudly. "You'll see everything… from up there." He began to climb the ladder.

"You want us to go up there?" Ellie said, horrified. She hated heights.

"It's the only way…we'll catch the giant," Thistle called down.

Noticing Ellie's anxious face, Jasmine put her arm round her. "It's okay, you can stay down here. Summer and I will look for him."

Ellie shook her head determinedly. "No, I'll do it."

"Just don't look down while you're climbing, Ellie," Summer suggested. "It might make you dizzy."

"I won't!" Ellie gulped.

Trixi whizzed up to the top of the flower on her leaf as Summer began to climb the ladder. Jasmine followed Summer, and Ellie came last of all. She clung to the rungs, looking straight ahead at the flower's smooth green stem and trying not to think about how high she was going.

As soon as Jasmine reached Thistle he

began to climb higher. "That's the way," he said. "We'll soon be at the top."

At last they reached the flower. Its daisy-like orange petals stretched out stiff and straight and Thistle clambered onto them. "Here we are," he said, stretching out his hand to Jasmine. She stepped off the ladder and onto the flower, then turned to help Summer.

They waited while Ellie climbed the last few rungs of the ladder. "Well done," said Summer as they helped her up onto the petals.

"You're perfectly safe up here," said Thistle with a smile.

Jasmine and Summer held Ellie's hands tightly as they looked out across the forest. Above them the sky was bright blue and cloudless, and just below a sea of flowers stretched away in all directions. They were every colour imaginable, with petals of many different shapes, some narrow and pointed, some frilly and others wide and flat.

"That one looks a bit like a tulip," Jasmine said, pointing to a pretty pink-and-yellow striped flower.

"And there are giant bluebells and

carnations over there," said Summer
eagerly.

Ellie gazed around in wonder, her fear
of being so high forgotten. "It's amazing.
All those different colours!" She made up
her mind to paint a picture of Wildflower
Wood when she got home.

"Is that sugarsap in the middle of the flowers, Thistle?" asked Jasmine. The sun was shining brightly up here and the liquid in the flowers' centres gleamed like pure gold.

"It is." He licked his lips. "And it's delicious!"

"It looks it!" agreed Jasmine.

"Can anyone see the giant?" asked Trixi.

They moved carefully around the petals, looking out in every direction. To their disappointment, the giant had completely vanished.

"Perhaps making him small wasn't such a good idea after all." Jasmine sighed. "He's probably hiding under some leaves."

"If we wait long enough my spell will

wear off," said Trixi, "and he'll grow big again. We should spot him easily enough then."

"Yes, but—" Summer began, then she broke off. "What's that?" She'd spotted something dark flapping above Wildflower Wood. It was a long way off and she narrowed her eyes to try to work out what it could be. "Are those birds?"

"It's Queen Malice's Storm Sprites!" gasped Ellie. "And they're carrying something."

They all stared hard, trying to see. "Whatever it is, it's wriggling like mad," said Summer.

"I think it's the giant!" Jasmine exclaimed suddenly. "They must be taking him to Queen Malice!"

"Let's get back down to the ground

and follow them," cried Ellie. She started down the ladder. "Come on, everyone!"

The girls and Thistle rushed back down the ladder. "They were going this way," Summer said, dashing along a broad path that seemed to be heading in the right direction.

Ellie and Jasmine followed close behind her. "I'm glad we're back on the ground." Ellie shuddered. "What a relief!"

"You did really well, Ellie," Jasmine said kindly.

They charged on through the forest, hoping they were still heading in the right direction. Then they heard angry shouting close by.

"Flap your wings faster, big ears!" screeched a harsh voice. "We have to get this giant to Queen Malice."

"Are you sure we've got the right person?" one of the sprites asked. "I thought giants were bigger than this."

"I am the giant!" the little giant squeaked.

"Told you so," the other sprite said, sticking out his tongue and blowing a raspberry.

"We're taking you to Queen Malice so she can tell you what to destroy next," the first sprite sniggered.

As they raced round a flower stem, the girls saw that the little giant had managed to drag the Storm Sprites almost down to the ground. They were still trying to fly away with him, but the giant was struggling so fiercely that they could hardly hold onto him. They flapped their bat-like wings furiously.

"Let go of me!"
squeaked the
giant. Swinging
his leg high,
he kicked one
of the Storm
Sprites on the
bottom.

"Ow!" it
squawked,
giving him a sharp shake.

"Serves you right," snapped another
sprite. "You should flap your wings
harder."

The girls couldn't help laughing. "This
is better than a comedy film," giggled
Ellie as the sprites struggled.

"Look!" Jasmine gasped. "What's
happening?" The air around the giant

was shimmering, though the Storm
Sprites didn't seem to have noticed yet.
They were still squabbling.

"I think my spell's wearing off," Trixi
gasped.

The girls looked at one another
anxiously as the giant began to grow.
His little legs stopped kicking in the air
and got longer and wider. Then his body
and head started to swell, bigger and
bigger…

The Storm Sprites were so busy arguing
they didn't notice. Two of them were
still tugging at his ears and the rest were
pulling his hair and nose when the giant
turned back into his enormous self, his
head towering above the trees.

"Uh oh!" one of the Storm Sprites
screeched, suddenly noticing what had

happened and letting go.

"What?" another replied, still pulling at the giant's hair. Then he turned and noticed the giant's huge frowning face.

"Argghhh!" the sprite yelled. Before he could get away the giant grabbed him.

"You caught me!" he roared. "You tried to take me away!"

"We were rescuing you," the Storm Sprite stuttered. "From those horrible humans." He jabbed a finger in the girls' direction, then grinned at the giant, showing his sharp teeth. "We're your friends."

"That's not true!" Summer yelled indignantly.

"I don't believe you!" the giant bellowed at the sprite.

"Quick, let's get out of here!" shrieked the other sprites. The cowardly creatures flapped away as fast as they could. But they couldn't fly quickly enough. The giant waved his hands, swatting them out of the air and sending them crashing into the flowers.

"Hah!" he shouted as he picked up the nearest sprite. "My friends, are you?

Hah!" He roared angrily.

The Storm Sprites got up and looked around dizzily, shaking their heads in confusion. "What happened?" one of them asked in a puzzled voice.

"Don't ask me!" snarled another. "But I bet it was all your fault!"

The giant stared down at the sprite in his fist, then sniffed him. "All this excitement has made me hungry," he roared.

"Oh no!" Summer gasped.

"Quick!" Ellie said. "Open the book!

Putting Things Right

The giant held the Storm Sprite by his foot so he was dangling upside down. "Fe, fi, fo, fum!" he growled. "I want a snack to fill my tum!"

"Put me down," moaned the sprite, his wings flapping uselessly. He covered his eyes with his hands and began to wail at the top of his voice.

"We've got to stop him!" Ellie gasped.
"The sprites might be horrid but we can't
let the giant eat them!"

Bravely, the girls ran up to the giant.
They stood right beside his massive foot,
trying not to think about what would
happen if he lifted it suddenly. Summer
opened the fairytale book and quickly
found the right page.

At once the book began to glow again.
A stream of sparkly yellow light poured
out of the picture and spiralled around
the giant, rising higher and higher until it
reached the top of his head.

Dropping the Storm Sprite, he tried to
slap the light away with his huge hands,
but it closed in tight around him like
coils of rope. "Get this horrible magic off
me!" he roared.

"It's working!" Jasmine cried eagerly as the giant began to shrink.

"Noooo!" he bellowed as the magic sucked him into the book. For a moment he looked up at the girls furiously, then he slipped into the empty space in the picture, a huge painted giant looming over a tiny village.

"There, Mr Giant," said Summer, shutting the book gently. "You're back where you belong."

"Hurray!" the girls cheered. They jumped up and down excitedly, then hugged one another, glad that the giant couldn't cause any more damage.

"Thank goodness he's out of the way!" Jasmine said, relieved.

"Yeah, but there are still five more fairytale baddies out there," called a sneering voice. "And you won't be so lucky with them!"

Glancing up, the girls saw the Storm Sprites looking down at them from the flower tops. Their spiky hair was squashed down flat after their encounter with the giant, and their wings were drooping tiredly.

"They'll be ready for you," another sprite jeered, his dark eyes glittering meanly. "And you won't stand a chance!"

"Would you like me to use pixie magic on them?" asked Trixi in a loud voice, winking at the girls. "I could make them teeny-tiny too, like the giant."

"No!" the Storm Sprites screeched. They flapped wildly away, barging one another aside in panic as they tried to get out of range.

The girls laughed. "I don't think they'll be back in a hurry," Ellie giggled.

Jasmine picked up the fairytale book. "We'll have to leave this here in the Secret Kingdom," she said, "so it's ready for us next time we come. Do you know a safe hiding place for it, Trixi?"

"I'll keep it," Trixi replied. She tapped her pixie ring and chanted:

> "Pixie magic, shrink this book
> So no one else can take a look."

The book began to glow again, this time with clear white light, dancing with silver and gold sparkles. Then it shrank until it was just a tiny square on the end of Jasmine's finger.

Trixi picked it up and slipped it into her pocket. "There," she said. "Nobody will find it now."

Suddenly they heard a sob. Looking round, the girls saw that Thistle had arrived. He was gazing sadly at the damage the giant had done. Flowers lay on their sides, their petals crumpled and

their sugarsap in puddles on the ground.
The houses in their stems had broken
windows and doors, and some of the
gnomes' things had fallen out when the
giant had tossed the flowers aside. There
was a smashed wardrobe a little way
away, and clothes had spilled out all
over the ground.

"This is terrible." Summer sighed. "The poor gnomes."

Jasmine looked hopefully at Trixi. "I don't suppose your pixie magic can fix the damage the giant's done, can it, Trixi?"

"I'll try," Trixi replied. She tapped her ring again and chanted:

"The forest looks a shocking sight –
Pixie magic, put things right!"

There was a sudden rush of wind that puffed purple mist through the forest. Vaguely, through the haze, the girls could make out the wind lifting the fallen flowers and planting them upright again. Then it whisked round the flower-stem houses and, as the mist cleared, they saw that the windows and doors were whole again.

"Thanks, Trixi!" the girls cried, glad that all the gnomes' homes were okay.

"Yes, thank you," said Thistle, drying his eyes.

Suddenly they heard a rustling sound behind them and whirled round, afraid that Queen Malice was creeping up on them. To their relief, they saw Thistle's gnome friends heading their way.

"We've come to thank you," one of them said, smoothing his beard and smiling happily. "Wildflower Wood is safe again because of you. And we can collect sugarsap for everyone in the Secret Kingdom to drink!"

A group of gnomes stepped forward holding three little cups made out of

curled petals. They were filled almost to
the brim with golden liquid. "Sugarsap,"
said Thistle proudly. "We thought you
might like to taste some."

"Yes, please!" the girls cried together.

"It smells amazing," said Summer. "Like candyfloss and toffee apples."

"And strawberries and cream," added Ellie. She took a sip. "Oh, it tastes brilliant!"

"Yummy!" Jasmine exclaimed, taking another sip. "That's the most delicious thing I've ever tasted in my whole life!"

"Definitely," agreed Summer. "I wish we could get it at home." She noticed suddenly that the sky was darkening and that a few stars were already twinkling between the flowers. "It's getting dark," she said.

Ellie and Jasmine looked up at the sky. "We've caught the giant, but the other fairytale baddies are still on the loose somewhere in the kingdom," Jasmine said.

"But we don't know where to look for them," Ellie pointed out.

"I'll send you a message as soon as I hear where one is," promised Trixi.

"Thank you." Jasmine smiled. "We'll come back as soon as we can."

Trixi kissed each of them on the tips of their noses. "Thank you for helping," she said.

Summer, Ellie and Jasmine joined

hands. Trixi tapped her ring and a whirlwind of pink sparks fizzed around the girls. "Goodbye," Ellie, Jasmine and Summer called.

Then the sparks closed in tight, blocking out Wildflower Wood and dazzling the girls with their brightness. They felt themselves being whisked upwards, then they landed gently in Jasmine's garden. The Magic Box was still on the lawn where they'd left it, and beside it were the daisy chains Ellie and Jasmine had been making.

"What an adventure!" breathed Jasmine.

"That giant was tricky to catch," Ellie said.

"But we managed it," Summer added proudly.

They looked at one another, their eyes shining with excitement. "Wildflower Wood was amazing, wasn't it?" said Jasmine. She picked up her daisy chain. "I'd forgotten about these."

Ellie picked hers up too. "Don't the flowers look tiny now?" she giggled.

"Yes!" Summer and Jasmine agreed, laughing.

"I hope we get to go back to the Secret Kingdom soon," Ellie said wistfully.

"I'm sure we will," said Jasmine. "There are five more fairytale baddies to catch, don't forget."

"I wonder where we'll go next," Ellie said.

The girls exchanged excited glances. They could hardly wait to find out.

In the next Secret Kingdom adventure, Ellie, Summer and Jasmine visit

Swan Palace

Read on for a sneak peek...

A New Adventure

"Just wait till I get my hands on you," sneered the evil enchanter in a bone-chilling voice. His eyes glinted as he held up a spellbook. "You'll be sorry you crossed me. Now come here!"

Summer Hammond let out a squeak of fright and hid her face in a pillow. She and her two best friends, Ellie and

Jasmine, were curled up on her bed watching a film together, and it was getting *very* scary! The characters in the film, Lauren and Sam, were trying to escape from a horrible wizard, and Summer couldn't bear to watch him chase them. She clutched her pillow as the enchanter gave a horrible gloating cackle. "What's happening?" she asked in a muffled voice.

Ellie giggled. "Summer! You're not really scared, are you? This is the most exciting bit!"

"Mwah-ha-ha!" cried Jasmine, copying the enchanter's cackle as she tossed her long black hair. "You'll be sorry you crossed me. Now come here!"

Summer squealed as first Jasmine and then Ellie began tickling her. The pillow fell off her head and she laughed helplessly. "Stop! Stop!" she shouted, feeling weak and breathless. "Help!"

Suddenly, all three of them toppled off the bed together with a bump and lay in a tangle on Summer's floor, still laughing.

"That baddie doesn't seem so scary any more," Summer giggled, struggling to a sitting position.

"Look – Lauren and Sam have escaped anyway," Ellie said, pointing at the screen. "Just like we got away from the giant in Wildflower Wood."

The girls fell silent for a moment, remembering their last exciting adventure in the Secret Kingdom. Ever since they'd found a mysterious Magic Box at their school fair, the girls had been special friends of the magical land, helping King Merry and his loyal subjects outwit his horrible sister Queen Malice, and had met the elves, brownies and other wonderful creatures living there.

The last time the girls had been whisked away to the Secret Kingdom, they'd discovered that Queen Malice was up to her trouble-causing ways again. Using her evil magic, Malice had cast a spell to unleash all the baddies from Summer's book of fairytales and sent them into the kingdom to cause chaos. The girls had helped stop an enormous giant from destroying Wildflower Wood, but they knew there were still five other villains somewhere out there.

Jasmine glanced over at the Magic Box, up on Summer's chest of drawers.

It was a wooden box with an oval mirror set into its lid, surrounded by six gleaming green gems. The sides of the box were decorated with beautiful carvings of mermaids, unicorns and other magical creatures, and inside was a collection of the special gifts the girls had been given during their adventures.

Jasmine went to pick up the box, then sat down on Summer's bed with it in her lap. "I wonder what's been happening in the Secret Kingdom since we were there," she said, gently running her fingers over the carvings...

Read

Swan Palace

to find out what
happens next!

Secret Kingdom

Have you read all the books in Series 3?

Wildflower Wood

ROSIE BANKS

Swan Palace

ROSIE BANKS

Snow Bear Sanctuary

ROSIE BANKS

Phoenix Festival

ROSIE BANKS

Fancy Dress Party

ROSIE BANKS

Jewel Tavern

ROSIE BANKS

Enjoy six sparkling adventures!

Secret Kingdom

Be in on the secret. Collect them all!

Enchanted Palace
ROSIE BANKS

Unicorn Valley
ROSIE BANKS

Cloud Island
ROSIE BANKS

Mermaid Reef
ROSIE BANKS

Magic Mountain
ROSIE BANKS

Glitter Beach
ROSIE BANKS

Series 1

When Jasmine, Summer and Ellie discover
the magical land of the Secret Kingdom,
a whole world of adventure awaits!

Secret Kingdom

Bubble Volcano

Sugarsweet Bakery

Dream Dale

Lily Pad Lake

Midnight Blaze

Fairytale Forest

Series 2

Wicked Queen Malice has cast a spell to
turn King Merry into a toad! Can the girls
find six magic ingredients to save him?

Secret Kingdom

Look out for the next sparkling series!

In Series 4,
meet the magical Animal Keepers of the
Secret Kingdom, who spread fun, friendship,
kindness and bravery throughout the land!

When wicked Queen Malice casts an evil spell
to reverse the Keepers' powers, it's up to Ellie,
Summer and Jasmine to find each animal's
magical charm and reunite them with their
Keeper – before their special values disappear
from the kingdom forever!

Available
February 2014

In **Puppy Fun**, Ellie, Summer and Jasmine must reunite the Puppy Keeper with his magical charm to make the Secret Kingdom fun again!

Can you find a way through the maze to reach the puppy? Watch out for Storm Sprites!

Secret Kingdom

Competition!

Evil Queen Malice has been up to no good again and hidden six of her naughty Storm Sprites in the pages of each Secret Kingdom book in series three!

Did you spot the Storm Sprite while you were reading this book?

Ellie, Summer and Jasmine need your help!

Can you find the pages where the cheeky Sprites are hiding in each of the six books in series three?

When you have found all six Storm Sprites, go online and tell us what pages they are hiding on and enter the competition at

www.secretkingdombooks.com

We will put all of the correct entries into a draw and select one winner to receive a special Secret Kingdom goodie bag featuring lots of sparkly gifts, including a glittery t-shirt!

Collect the tokens from each Secret Kingdom book to get special Secret Kingdom gifts!

In every Secret Kingdom book there are three Friendship Tokens that you can exchange for special gifts! Save up all the tokens from the back of the books. Once you've collected 18, send them in to us to get a bumper goodie bag of activities and gifts!

Surprise goodies inside!

To take part in this offer, please send us a letter telling us why you like Secret Kingdom books so much! Don't forget to:

1) Include your name and address
2) Include the signature of a parent or guardian

Send your tokens to:
Secret Kingdom Friendship Token Offer
Orchard Books Marketing Department
338 Euston Road, London, NW1 3BH

Closing date: 29th November 2013

Terms and Conditions
(1) Open to UK and Republic of Ireland residents only (2) Purchase of the Secret Kingdom books is necessary (3) Please get the signature of your parent/guardian to enter this offer (4) The correct number of tokens must be included for the offer to be redeemed (5) Photocopied tokens will not be accepted (6) Prizes are distributed on a first come, first served basis whilst stocks last (7) No part of the offer is exchangeable for cash or any other offer (8) Please allow 28 days for delivery (9) We will use your data only for the purpose of fulfilling this offer (10) Prizes may vary from pictures shown. We reserve the right to offer prizes of an alternative or greater value.

www.secretkingdombooks.com

1 Friendship Token	1 Friendship Token	1 Friendship Token
www.secretkingdombooks.com	www.secretkingdombooks.com	www.secretkingdombooks.com

Secret Kingdom

A magical world of friendship and fun!

Join best friends Ellie, Summer and Jasmine at

www.secretkingdombooks.com

and enjoy games, sneak peeks and lots more!

You'll find great activities, competitions, stories
and games, plus a special newsletter for
Secret Kingdom friends!